Shaggy Dog's CHRISTMAS

written and illustrated by Donald Charles

℗ CHILDRENS PRESS™

CHICAGO

For Frannie, Lluvia, and Jesse

Library of Congress Cataloging in Publication Data

Charles, Donald.
    Shaggy Dog's Christmas.

    Summary: Shaggy Dog follows his list of things to do
for Christmas
    [1. Dogs—Fiction.   2.   Christmas—Fiction]
I.   Title.
PZ7.C374Sd   1985   [E]   85-14972
ISBN 0-516-03675-0   AACR2

Shaggy Dog's CHRISTMAS

Shaggy Dog
has a list
of things
to do for
Christmas.

1-SHOP

Shaggy Dog buys
crayons, and cloth,
and yarn so he can
make gifts for
his friends.

2-MAKE PRESENTS

"I'll make ear-warmers for Mouse and Rabbit," says Shaggy Dog.

3-WRAP

Shaggy Dog is
wrapping the
gifts for
his friends.

11

4-SEND CARDS

Shaggy Dog
made some
Christmas
cards.

14

5-VISIT SANTA

"Please bring me
a warm hat, and
some skates," says
Shaggy Dog.

6-DECORATE

"It's time to
trim the
Christmas
tree," says
Shaggy Dog.

Shaggy Dog puts lots of tinsel
and ornaments on the tree.

"That's just perfect," says Shaggy Dog.

7-BAKE

Shaggy Dog loves
Christmas cookies.

8-SING

Shaggy Dog
and his friends
are singing
Christmas carols.

9-HANG STOCKING

Shaggy Dog
hangs up his
stocking on
Christmas Eve.

10-PLAY

"Look what Santa brought," shouts Shaggy Dog on Christmas morning.

Shaggy Dog has
a Christmas list.
Do you?

1-SHOP

2-MAKE PRESENTS

3-WRAP

4-SEND CARDS

5-VISIT or WRITE SANTA

6-DECORATE

7-BAKE

8-SING

9-HANG STOCKING

10-PLAY

ABOUT THE AUTHOR / ARTIST

Donald Charles started his long career as an artist and author more than twenty-five years ago after attending the University of California and the Art League School of California. He began by writing and illustrating feature articles for the *San Francisco Chronicle,* and also sold cartoons and ideas to *The New Yorker* and *Cosmopolitan* magazines. Since then he has been, at various times, a longshoreman, ranch hand, truck driver, and editor of a weekly newspaper, all enriching experiences for a writer and artist. Ultimately he became creative director for an advertising agency, a post which he resigned several years ago to devote himself full-time to book illustration and writing. Mr. Charles has received frequent awards from graphic societies, and his work has appeared in numerous textbooks and periodicals.

NOTE TO PARENT / LIBRARIAN / TEACHER

The Shaggy Dog and Calico Cat series fill a specific niche in the storybook genre. Ideal for headstart programs, the minimal text invites the non-reader to begin word recognition. Each book starts with the premise that the reader is being introduced to the subject matter for the first time. Basic concepts are presented in each story in an entertaining, non-textbook approach. With the continuity carried principally in the illustration, the stories have proved to be an effective incentive to the beginning reader.